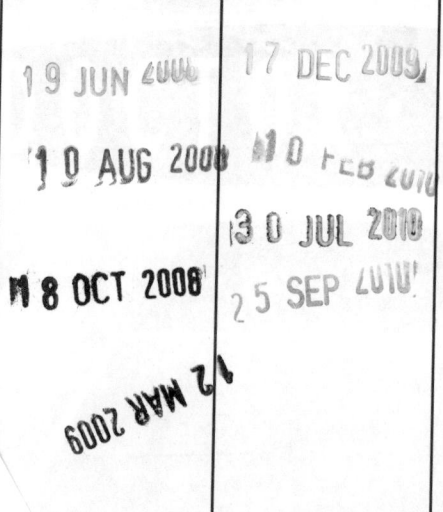

...book should be returned/renewed by
...est date shown above. Overdue items
...arges which prevent self-service
...Please contact the library.

...rth Libraries
...newal Hotline
...8
...dsworth.gov.uk

Wandsworth

CAPTAIN JACK

BBC CHILDREN'S BOOKS
Published by the Penguin Group
Penguin Books Ltd, 80 Strand, London, WC2R 0RL, England
Penguin Group (USA), Inc., 375 Hudson Street, New York, New York 10014, USA
Penguin Books (Australia) Ltd, 250 Camberwell Road, Camberwell, Victoria 3124, Australia.
(A division of Pearson Australia Group Pty Ltd)
Canada, India, New Zealand, South Africa.
Published by BBC Children's Books, 2007
Text and design © Children's Character Books, 2007
Images © BBC 2004
Written by Justin Richards.
10 9 8 7 6 5 4 3 2 1
Printed in China.
ISBN-13: 978-1-40590-311-0
ISBN-10: 1-40590-311-2

DOCTOR · WHO

CAPTAIN JACK

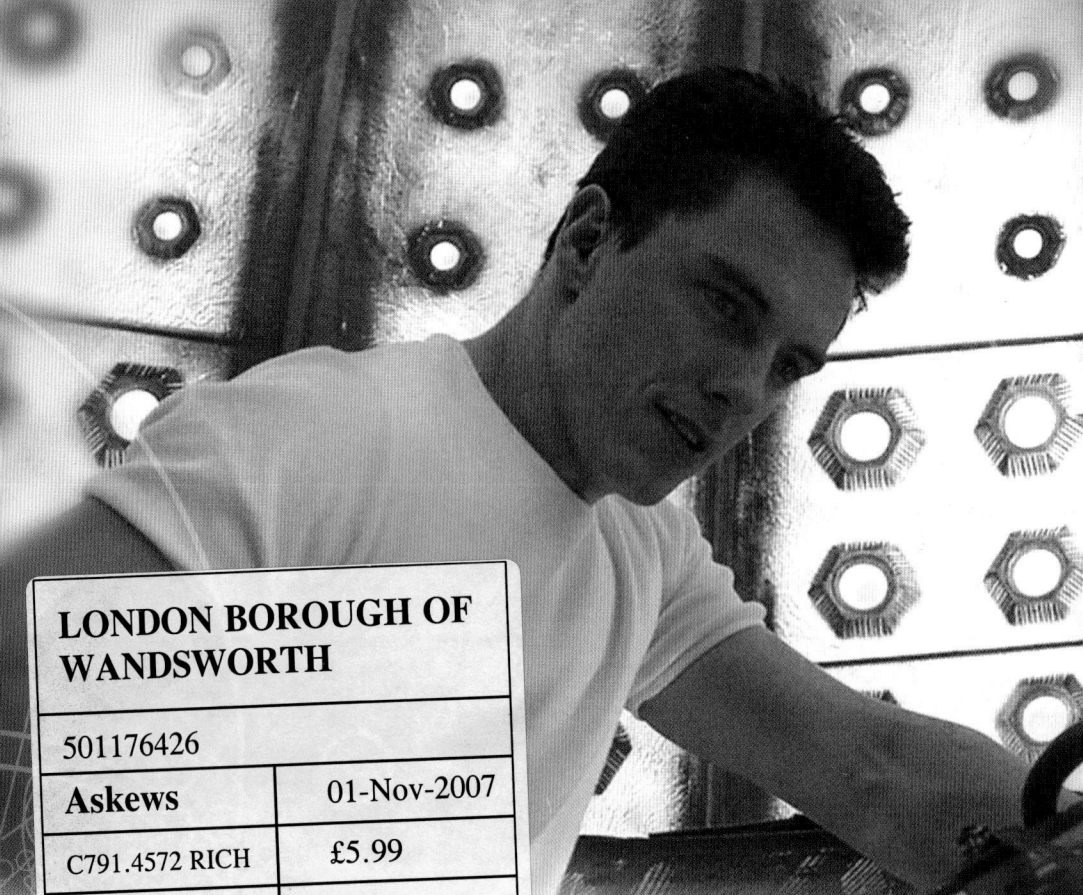

BBC CHILDREN'S BOOKS
Published by the Penguin Group
Penguin Books Ltd, 80 Strand, London, WC2R 0RL, England
Penguin Group (USA), Inc., 375 Hudson Street, New York, New York 10014, USA
Penguin Books (Australia) Ltd, 250 Camberwell Road, Camberwell, Victoria 3124, Australia.
(A division of Pearson Australia Group Pty Ltd)
Canada, India, New Zealand, South Africa.
Published by BBC Children's Books, 2007
Text and design © Children's Character Books, 2007
Images © BBC 2004
Written by Justin Richards.
10 9 8 7 6 5 4 3 2 1

Printed in China.
ISBN-13: 978-1-40590-311-0
ISBN-10: 1-40590-311-2

CONTENTS

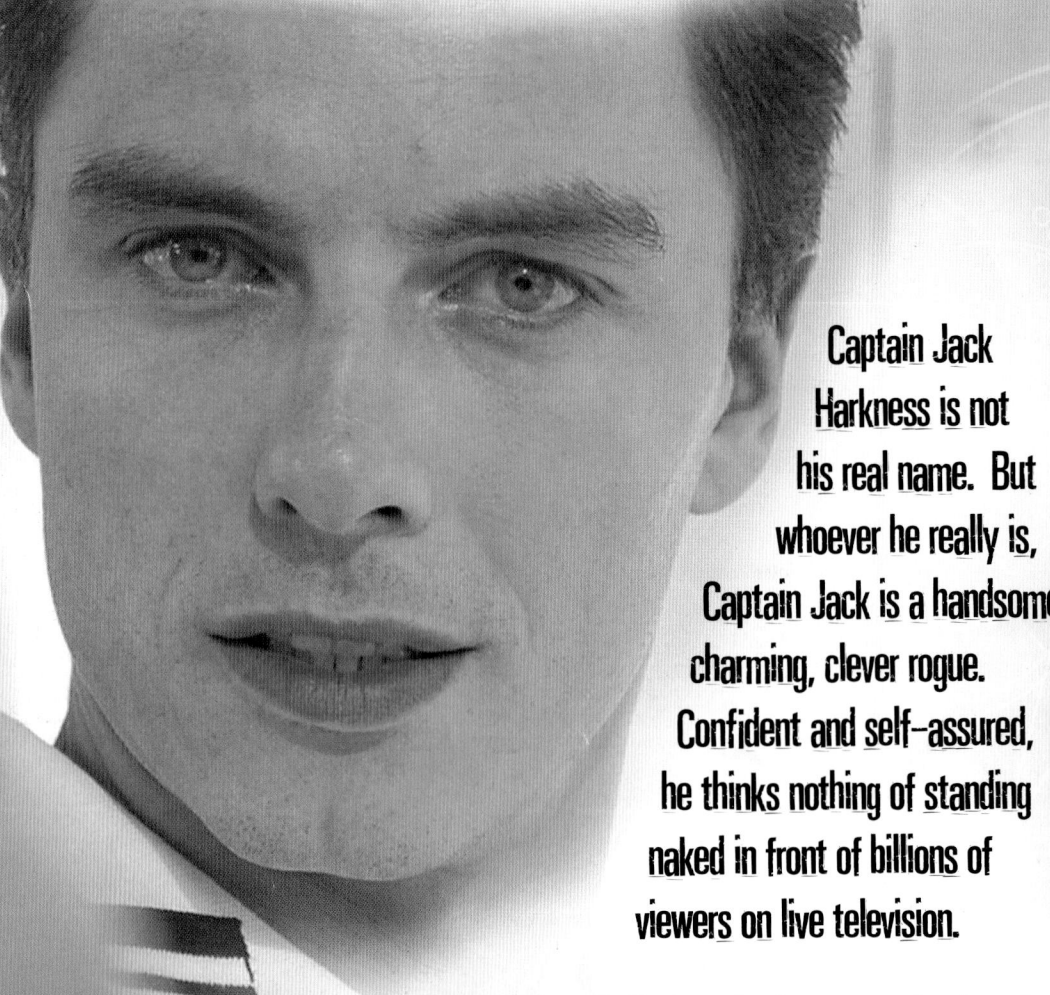

MEET CAPTAIN JACK

Captain Jack Harkness is not his real name. But whoever he really is, Captain Jack is a handsome, charming, clever rogue. Confident and self-assured, he thinks nothing of standing naked in front of billions of viewers on live television.

He used to be a Time Agent, probably from the 51st century, but he quit after they stole two years of his memories — and he wants them back. After that he made his own way in the universe, relying on his wits and charm, and his skill as a con man.

When the Doctor and Rose first met Captain Jack, his plan was to find some space junk, allow a Time Agent to track it to Earth and then convince the Agent it was valuable. Once Jack had a finder's fee, the junk would be destroyed by a German bomb, so the Agent would never discover it was a con.

But after the Doctor and Rose saved him from his spaceship which was about to explode, Jack became something of a reformed character. He helped them sort out a Slitheen hiding in Cardiff, and organised the defence of the Game Station against an army of Daleks. But when he was exterminated, it seems his adventure may have just been beginning…

Name:	Unknown
Alias:	Captain Jack Harkness
Species:	Unknown, possibly human
Height:	1.85m (6'1")
Hair:	Dark
Eyes:	Hazel
Age:	Apparently about 35. Actually over 150.
Home Planet:	Unknown, possibly Earth or one of its colonies.
Professions:	Time Agent, Con Man, Investigator, Adventurer…

Tall and handsome — looking good for over 150 years old!

Often wears military great coat

Vortex Manipulator — enables Jack to survive in the Time Vortex

Even if Jack's heart stops, he doesn't die

Mr Sutton, the overseer, had been in charge of the Clarendon Workhouse since 1895. Two years into the job and he reckoned he was doing well. He knew almost all the children by name. He recognised the voice of Anthony Bradshaw coming from the long dormitory. Why wasn't the boy outside in the yard with the other kids?

Sutton's boots clicked on the bare boards as he approached the bed where the boy was sitting, silent now. He looked like he'd been crying. Well, most of them cried – missing homes they no longer had, parents and friends who were long gone.

'What's up?' Sutton asked. 'Why aren't you outside? And who were you talking to?'

The boy's eyes caught the dusty sunlight as he looked up at Sutton. 'No one,' he answered.

'Worked that out,' Sutton said gently. 'There's no one else here. But you were talking.'

Anthony looked away. 'I was talking to my friend,' he said

quietly. 'My best friend. My best friend ever.'

The man was wearing a long, dark grey coat even though it was a warm evening. He cut an impressive figure – tall, self-assured, handsome and charming – as he ordered a glass of wine at the theatre bar.

'Captain Jack Harkness,' he told the young woman who was staring at him. He switched on a smile. 'Can I get you something?'

'I'm with my father,' she said, apologetic and disappointed.

'Maybe I can get you both something.' Jack smiled again. Then he remembered why he was here, and the smile faded. 'Another time maybe.' He raised his glass to her. 'I'm sort of on duty.'

Jack didn't usually spend time at the music hall, but there was an act he was interested in. Professionally interested in. He had a private box to himself, and was stretched out comfortably across two chairs when the boy came on stage.

'The Amazing Anthony – The Wonder of 1898,' Jack read off the board at the side of the stage as he sat up and peered through a small pair of binoculars at the two people below.

The boy looked ill. He was maybe ten years old and his face was pale and drawn as he sat on an upright chair, not seeming to listen to the older man who was doing the talking. Edward Hardiman claimed to be the boy's uncle. He had thinning grey hair and a suit that had seen better days. But by all accounts the act was popular and gaining a lot of attention. Hardiman was explaining to the audience

what Jack had already been told.

The boy – the Amazing Anthony – could foretell the future. He'd spoken of a coming war – a conflict in which hundreds of thousands would die. He'd said that in a hundred years machines would exist that could perform millions of calculations in a fraction of a second. It was a good act. Jack hoped it was an act.

'A hundred guineas,' Hardiman declared. He held up what might have been a wad of banknotes. 'I say again, a hundred guineas to anyone who can ask Amazing Anthony a question he cannot answer. It's an offer I've made every night for nearly a month. And I still have my hundred guineas. Yes sir!' He pointed to a woman who was waving from the audience. 'I warn you, only ask a question if you are sure you want to know the answer – we've had some embarrassed people this past month!'

'When's my birthday?' the woman asked.

The boy looked up, his eyes wide and nervous through Jack's

binoculars. He looked bored as much as anything. 'July 25th,' he said, his thin voice carrying through the hushed theatre. '1857,' he added.

'She told me she was twenty-one!' the man sitting with the woman announced, pretending to be outraged. The woman slapped him, and the audience laughed.

'Anyone else?' the man on stage asked.

'How's he do it?' someone shouted out.

'How indeed?' Jack asked himself.

There was silence for a moment, then Anthony replied: 'I have explained before. I have a friend. An invisible friend. He is always with me, and no one else can see him. I know little, but my friend knows everything and tells me the answers. You can't hear him – only I can.'

'What's your friend's name?' another voice shouted.

Jack hardly heard. He was leaning over the edge of the box, staring down at the stage. Examining the two figures in the middle of the bare boards, and the way the spotlights cast their shadows against

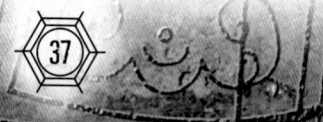

the curtain at the back of the stage. A trick of the light, perhaps? There were three shadows.

'My friend's name is Lawphoram.'

And Jack blinked. 'Of course.'

He leaped to his feet, yelling above the sound of the people below all wanting a go. 'I have a question. And I'm going to win a hundred guineas.'

'Very well,' Hardiman shouted back. 'The confident American gentleman in the box. Yes, sir – what is your question? But I warn you, the money will not be yours.'

'I think it will,' Jack told him. 'Tell me, Anthony – and I really want to know this… How will I die?'

The audience was silent. The boy looked confused. He shook his head, seemed to be listening. Then, finally he spoke. His voice so quiet it barely carried. Hardiman's mouth dropped open in surprise.

'Didn't catch that,' Jack shouted. 'What did you say, Anthony? Tell me – how will I die?'

The boy looked up at him – his eyes wide and sad and scared, and his voice nervous and strained.

'I don't know,' he said.

'Uncle' Edward Hardiman didn't have a hundred guineas. Anthony's act earned a lot of money, but Hardiman spent it almost as fast as it came in on drink and on gambling. Jack was happy

to agree to meet after the show was over to collect his winnings. But he wasn't foolish enough really to wait until after the show.

Which was why he was standing outside the back door of the theatre just minutes after the act was over when Hardiman bundled poor pale Anthony out.

'Thought I might find you here,' Jack said.

Hardiman tried to run for it. He didn't get far. Jack slammed him into the brick wall and held him tight. 'Let me guess – no hundred guineas?' Hardiman couldn't answer as Jack's forearm was tight across his throat. 'Well, that's just fine. Because, you know what? I don't want a hundred guineas.'

Jack released his hold and Hardiman collapsed to the damp pavement. Anthony watched without comment.

'Guess you knew that already, kid,' Jack said as he helped Hardiman back to his feet. 'But don't even try to run for it. Your uncle wouldn't like that, I'm guessing. I'm guessing too that the voice in your head – your friend Lorphoram – is screaming at you to get away. Because he knows what's coming next, doesn't he?' Jack reached out and grabbed Anthony by the wrist, pulling him close. 'Except he isn't a "he". He's an "it". And a very nasty it at that.'

'What do you want?' Hardiman stammered. 'If not money, then – what?'

'I want the boy,' Jack said, feeling Anthony try to pull free, but holding on tight. 'And don't give me any rubbish about how he's family and you're responsible and you care. Because that's just not true is it?'

'I can't let you – '

Jack glared at the man. 'You bought this poor kid from a Workhouse overseer in Clarendon Street last year. Like a slave. Well, you owe me a hundred guineas so I reckon you've turned a tidy profit. Now – scram!'

Hardiman looked into Jack's eyes. He saw the depth of the anger and emotion there. And he scrammed.

'What are you going to do to me?'
Anthony said when Hardiman had gone.
Jack let go of the boy's wrist and
stood facing him. 'I'm going to help
you.' He reached out both his
hands and cradled the
boy's head between
them, looking
intently at him.
'That voice in
your head is
an alien. It's
a creature
of energy,
or thought,
from another

world. Oh yeah, it's called a Lawphoram, it was telling the truth about that. But not about much else.'

'Another world?' Anthony looked even more pale than usual. 'Why can't anyone else see him – it? Why only me?'

'Because it's inside your mind. There's the ghost of an image, outside the range of human sight and perception. But most of it is inside you, feeding. And you know what it feeds on – what keeps it alive?'

Jack took away his hands, allowing Anthony to shake his head. His voice was a frightened whisper: 'What?'

'You. It feeds on thought. On your mind. That's how it knows. It knows about the future because it's from the future – it fell to Earth from the vortex. Don't know why. Maybe it got caught up in someone else's war, who knows? But it's here now. In you. It can sense the energy in the minds of the people who ask you questions and it can see the answers in there too. It's a gift.'

'A curse,' the boy muttered.

'You know, you're not wrong.' Jack pulled back the sleeve of his coat. There was something strapped to his wrist – a strange, chunky bracelet-like device. 'I said it feeds on you, and I meant that. It's eating you up, Anthony – eating your thoughts. You'll waste away and die. Unless I get it out of there.'

Jack turned a small wheel on the side of the device. He stepped closer to Anthony.

'Please…' the boy said.

'Is it screaming yet?' Jack turned the wheel further – right the way around.

And Anthony Bradshaw collapsed. His eyelids flickered as Jack lifted the small child and cradled him in his arms. The boy's face was already getting some colour back.

'You'll be all right,' Jack whispered. 'I promise – you'll be all right.'

The old man looked up from the threadbare armchair beside his narrow bed. His eyes were pale and moist with age. He struggled to focus on the figure standing beside him.

'Jack?'

'Anthony – how's it going?'

'Is it really you? I thought I was dreaming. Come a bit closer – my eyes aren't so good these days.'

'This better?' The figure leaned down towards him.

And it was Jack – exactly as he had been, all those years ago. 'You – you haven't changed,' Anthony Bradshaw said in surprise

Jack laughed. 'Oh, I've changed,' he said. 'I just look the same.'

Anthony smiled and nodded. 'And did you ever find out?' He took Jack's hand and held it tight. 'Did you ever get an answer to your question – the question you asked me that night at the theatre?'

'No,' Jack said quietly. 'But I didn't expect to.' He straightened up. 'You see, I know now – and I knew then, though I didn't want to believe it – I don't die.' Then, even quieter: 'Only my friends.'

Anthony could feel himself slipping away, back into sleep. He slept so much these days. But he'd had a good life – such a very good life, once it got properly started. He knew who to thank for that. He could hear Jack walking slowly away, towards the door.

'Have you come…' Anthony said as he drifted into sleep again, 'have you come to say…'

A whisper from the doorway: 'Goodbye.'

The nurse tucked the blanket round Anthony and settled him for the night.

'I thought I heard you talking to someone earlier,' she said. 'Only, there's no one

else here.' She hesitated by the bed. 'But you were talking.'

Anthony looked away. 'I was talking to my friend,' he said quietly. 'My best friend. My best friend ever.'

DOCTOR · WHO

OTHER GREAT FILES TO COLLECT

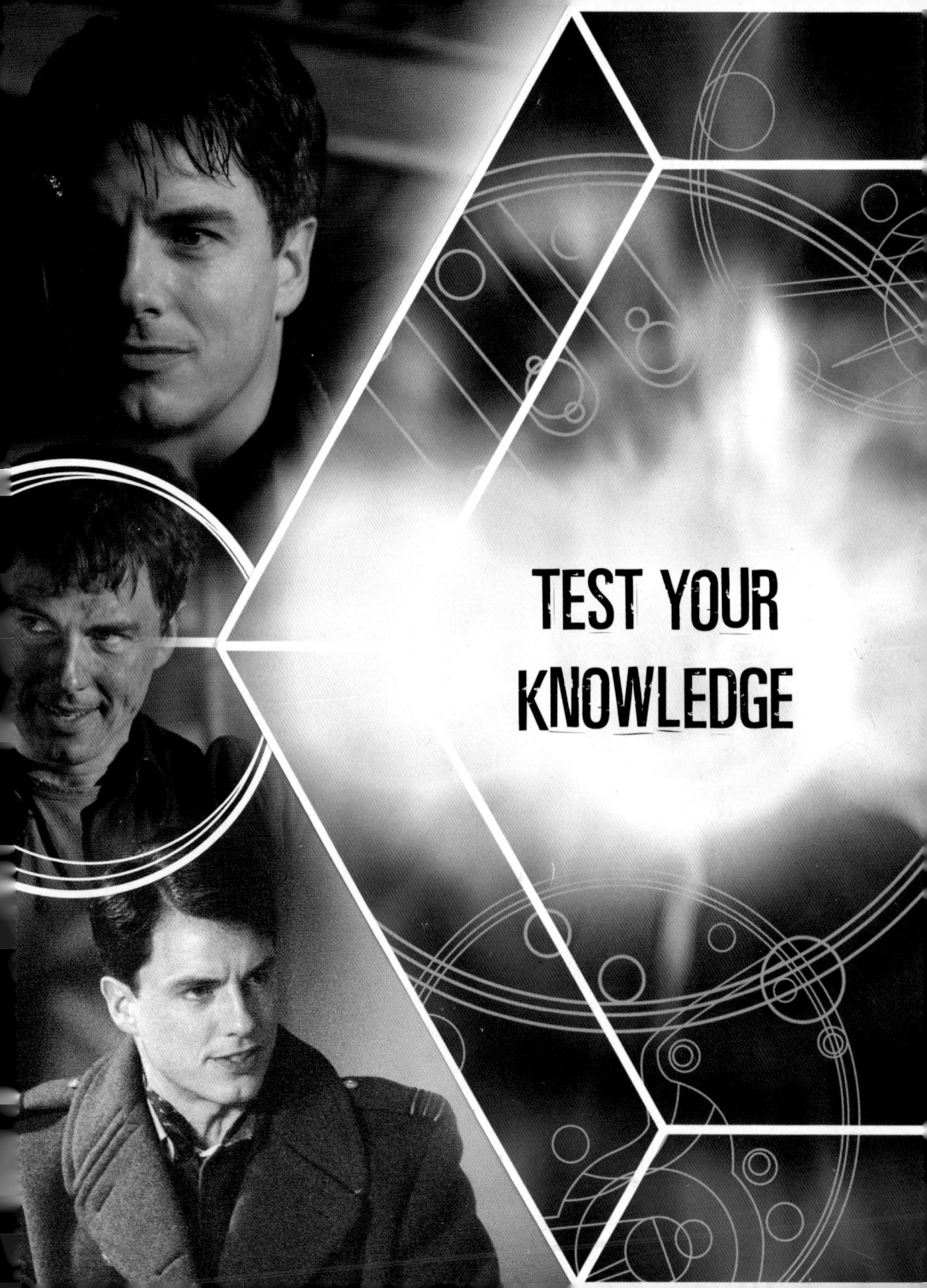

TEST YOUR KNOWLEDGE

THE DOCTOR

When Jack first met the Doctor and Rose he thought they were Time Agents and tried to con them into buying a Chula Warship. But as they worked together to solve the mystery of the Empty Child they became friends. The Doctor is the last of the Time Lords, a powerful race who were destroyed in the Time War. A Time Lord can save himself from death by changing every cell in his body — this is called regeneration. After Jack was left behind on the Game Station, the Doctor was forced to regenerate — so when they meet again on the planet Malcassairo he doesn't appear to be the same man. But Jack knew it was the Doctor.

OSE TYLER

ose travelled with the Doctor when he first
et Captain Jack. Rose and Captain Jack became
ood friends after he rescued her from hanging
nder a barrage balloon as the German air force
rrived to attack London. They became such good
iends that the Doctor even got a bit jealous.

hen Jack was exterminated by the Daleks, Rose brought him back to life. Using the power of
e Time Vortex she was able to save him, and now he cannot die! Jack remembers Rose fondly.
hen he found himself back on Earth in Rose's past, a couple of times in the 1990s he went
ck to the Powell Estate where she grew up. But he never spoke to her.

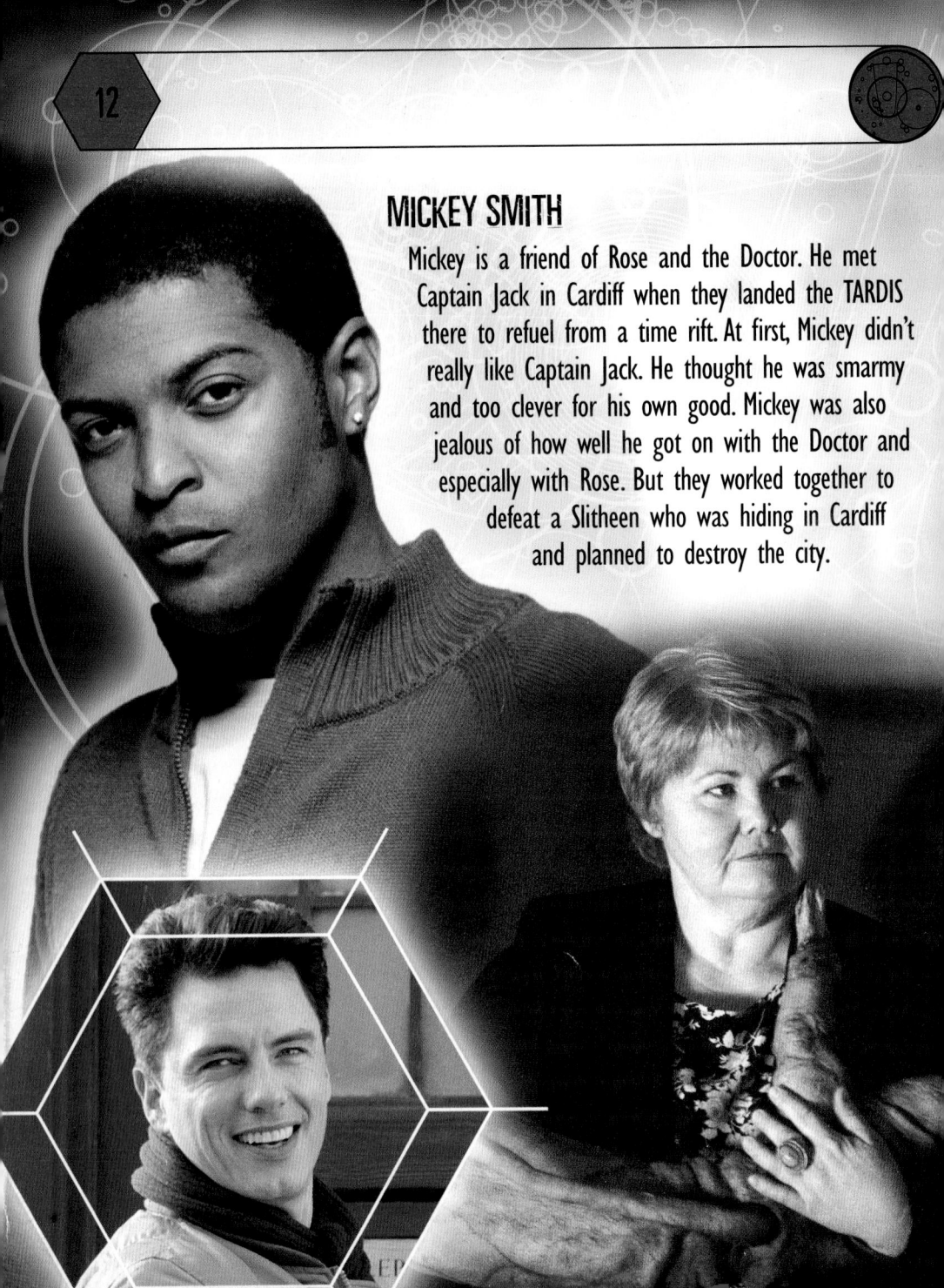

MICKEY SMITH

Mickey is a friend of Rose and the Doctor. He met Captain Jack in Cardiff when they landed the TARDIS there to refuel from a time rift. At first, Mickey didn't really like Captain Jack. He thought he was smarmy and too clever for his own good. Mickey was also jealous of how well he got on with the Doctor and especially with Rose. But they worked together to defeat a Slitheen who was hiding in Cardiff and planned to destroy the city.

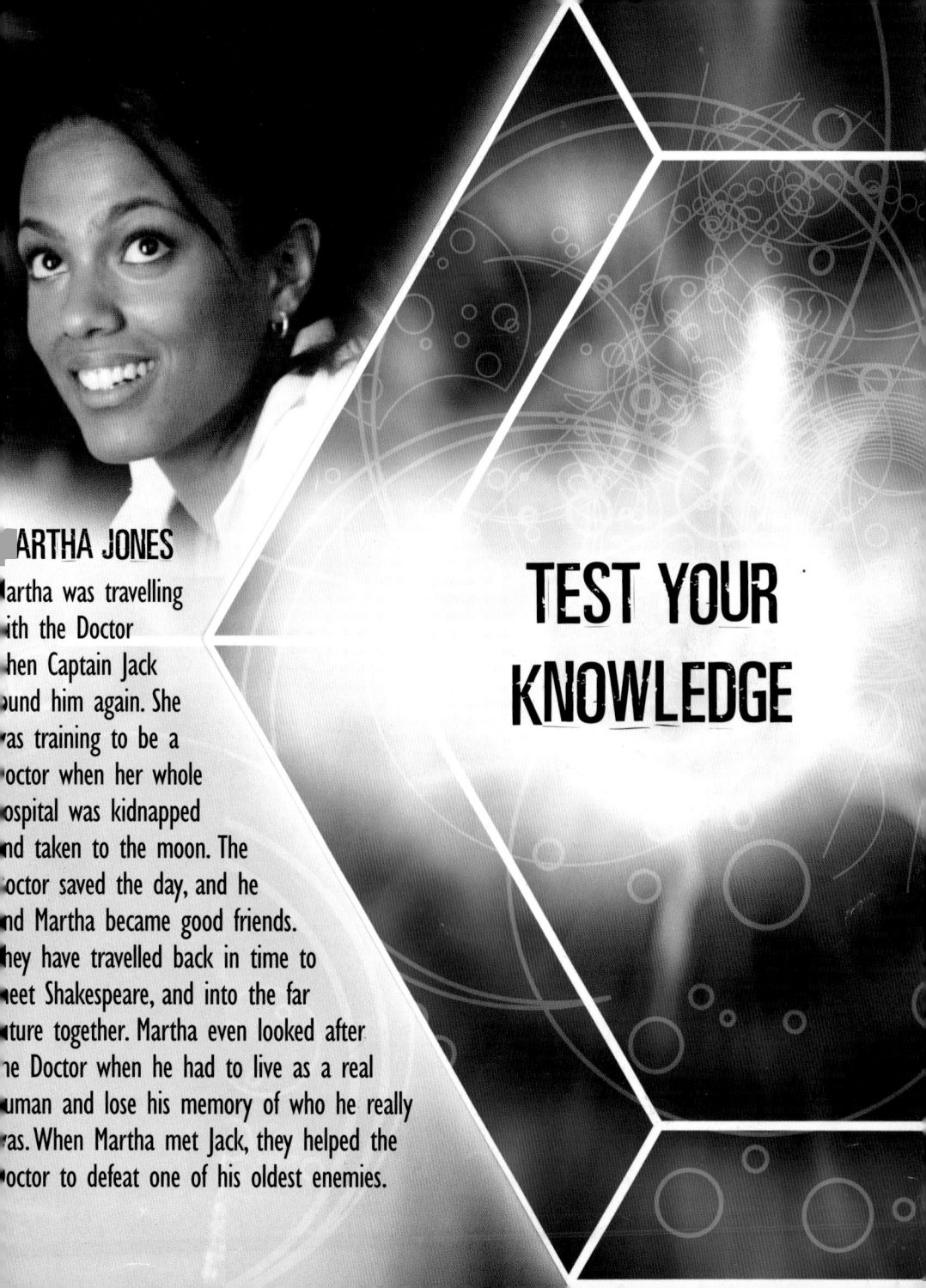

MARTHA JONES

Martha was travelling with the Doctor when Captain Jack found him again. She was training to be a doctor when her whole hospital was kidnapped and taken to the moon. The Doctor saved the day, and he and Martha became good friends. They have travelled back in time to meet Shakespeare, and into the far future together. Martha even looked after the Doctor when he had to live as a real human and lose his memory of who he really was. When Martha met Jack, they helped the Doctor to defeat one of his oldest enemies.

TEST YOUR KNOWLEDGE

14 CAPTAIN JACK'S ENEMIES

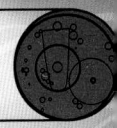

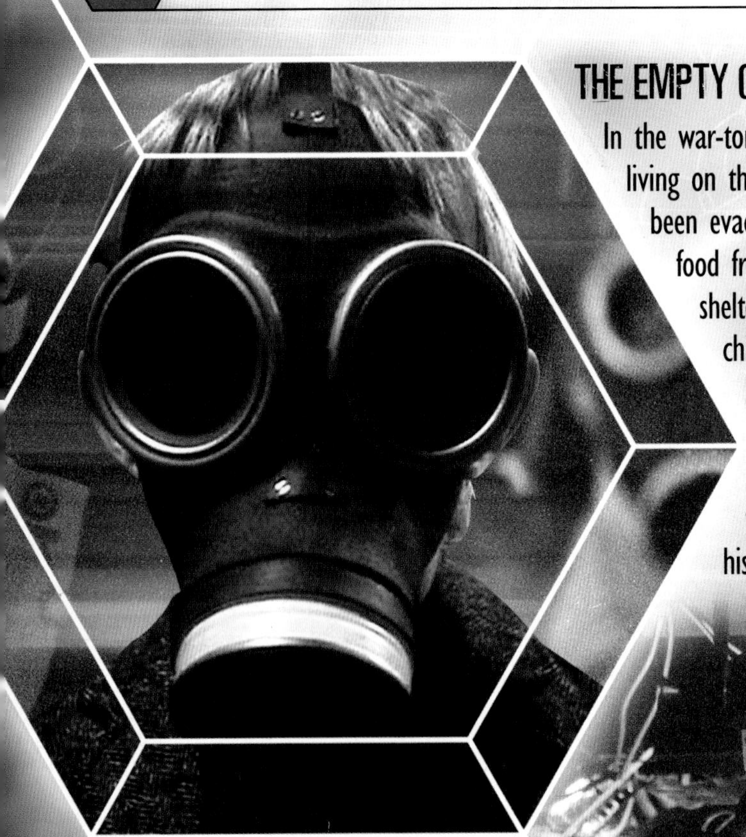

THE EMPTY CHILD

In the war-torn Britain of 1941, the children living on the streets (who should have been evacuated out of London) stole food from the houses of people sheltering from air raids. The other children regarded Nancy as their leader. But they were haunted by another child - a small boy wearing a gas mask, who was always asking for his mummy.

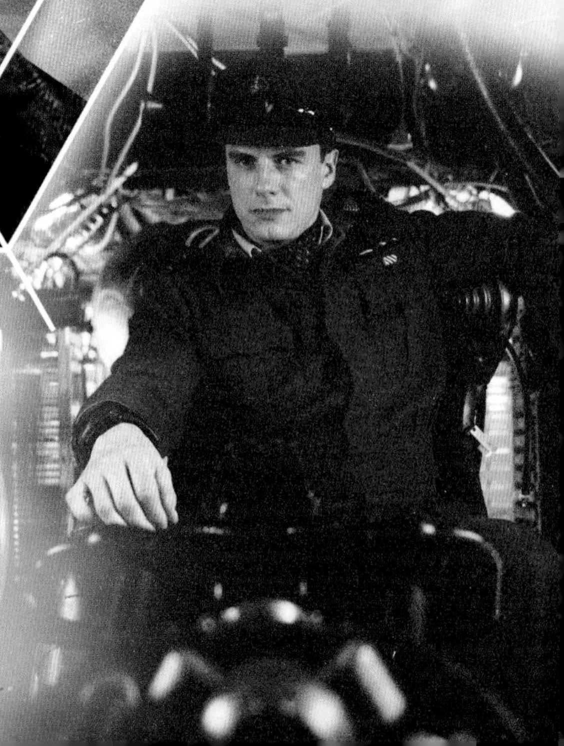

The mysterious child could project his voice through the TARDIS telephone, a radio and even a music box. Captain Jack didn't realise that it was all his fault because of the nanogenes in the Chula ambulance, but in the end the Doctor saved the day and everyone was all right.

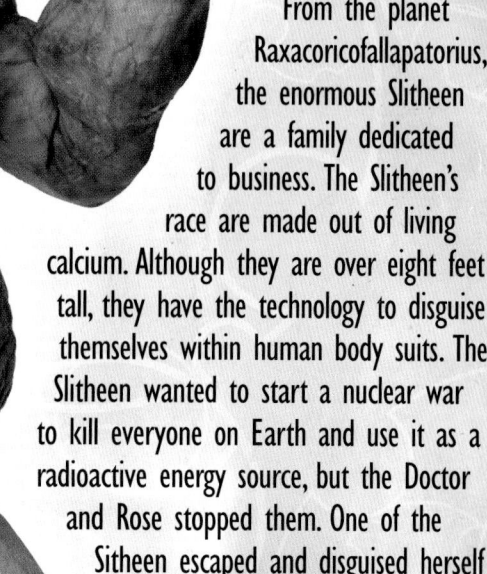

THE SLITHEEN

From the planet Raxacoricofallapatorius, the enormous Slitheen are a family dedicated to business. The Slitheen's race are made out of living calcium. Although they are over eight feet tall, they have the technology to disguise themselves within human body suits. The Slitheen wanted to start a nuclear war to kill everyone on Earth and use it as a radioactive energy source, but the Doctor and Rose stopped them. One of the Sitheen escaped and disguised herself as Margaret Blaine, the Mayor of Cardiff. Captain Jack helped the Doctor and his friends stop her from destroying the city.

THE DALEKS

Hated and feared throughout the whole universe, the Daleks are the most ruthless and evil creatures in all creation. They might look like robots, but inside that protective, armoured shell is a living creature.

The Daleks are so dangerous and evil that the Doctor's own people — the Time Lords — tried to go back to before their creation and stop them ever existing. As a result, the Daleks and the Time Lords have been the deadliest of enemies and fought a great Time War in which both sides seemed to be wiped out.

ut the Daleks survived, and they are out to
xterminate everyone and everything — especially
heir greatest enemy, the last of the Time
ords: the Doctor.

Vhen the Dalek army attacked the Game
tation, the Doctor put Captain Jack in
harge of fighting against them.
le managed to hold the Daleks
ack for a while — but then he
as exterminated...

TEST YOUR
KNOWLEDGE

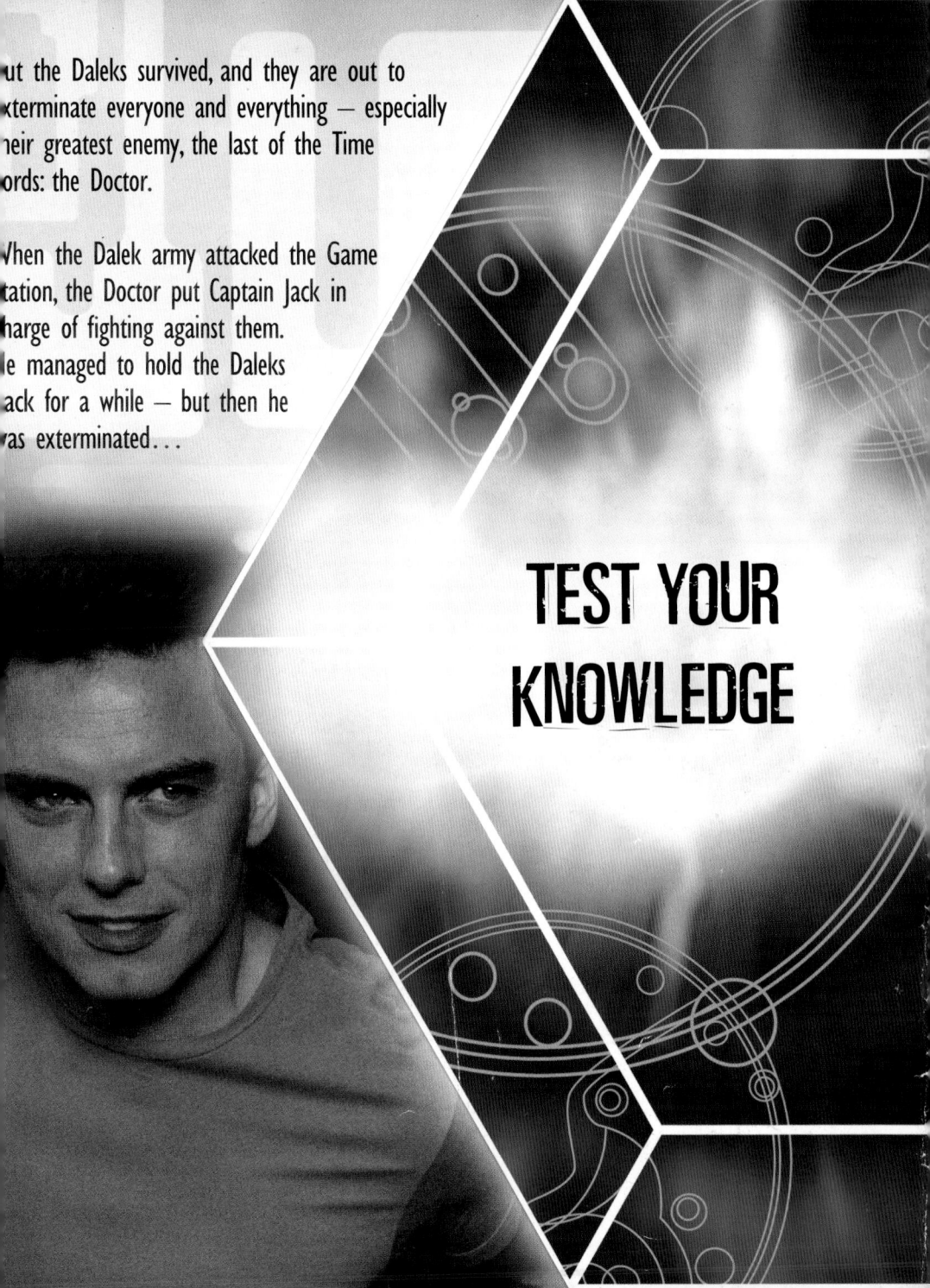

MYSTERIOUS CON MAN

When the Doctor and Rose first met Captain Jack Harkness he was in 1941, masquerading as an American volunteer in the RAF's 133 Squadron. Thinking the Doctor and Rose were Time Agents, he tried to sell them a Chula Warship. Only it wasn't actually a warship but an ambulance — Jack planned to blow it up before anyone found out. But the nanogenes — tiny little medical robots — from the ship had escaped and got out of control. They tried to turn everyone into a gas mask zombie. Luckily the Doctor was able to sort it all out and everyone was OK.

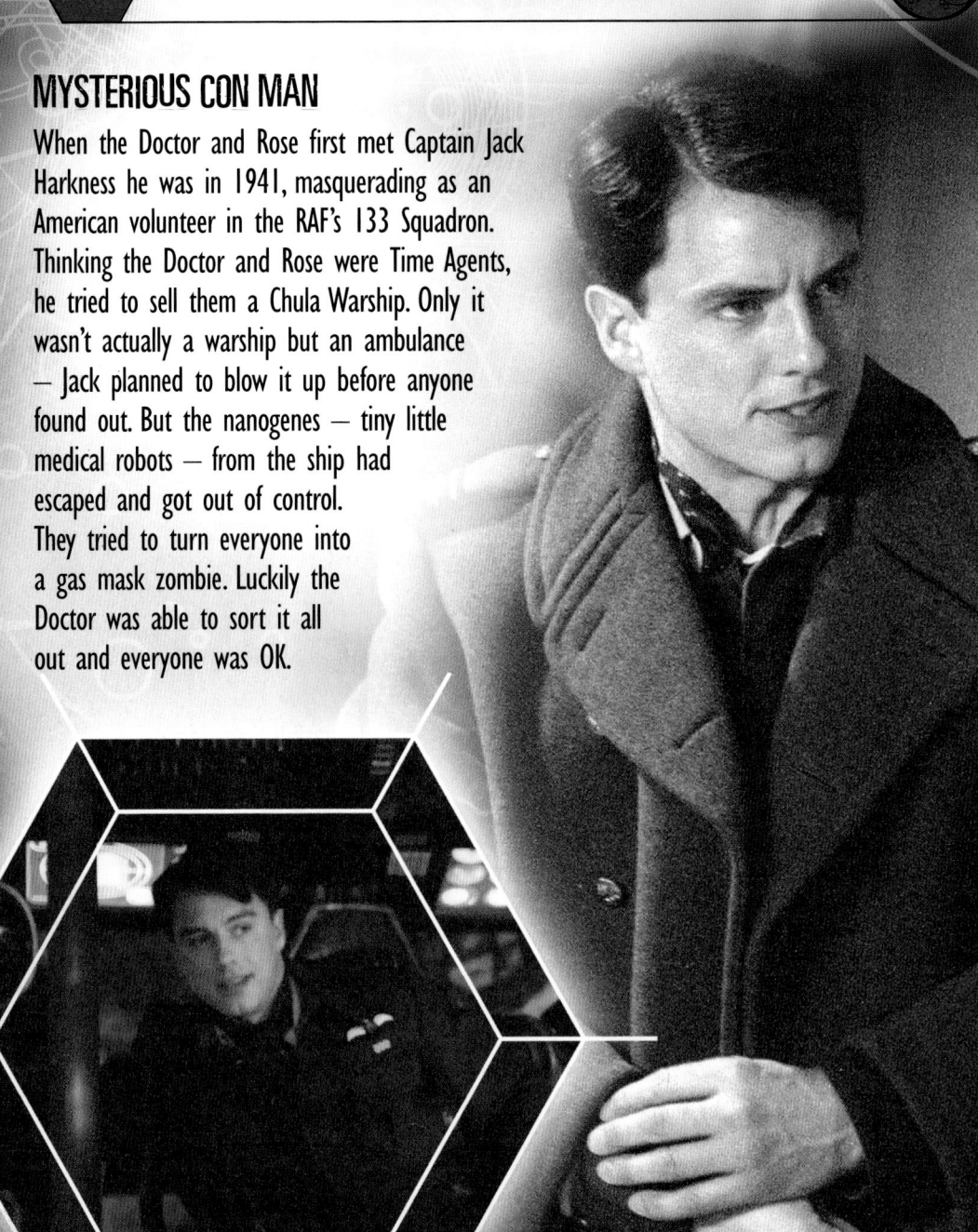

Jack risked his own life to stop a German bomb landing on the Chula Ship, and thought he was going to die when it exploded in his ship. But the Doctor and Rose arrived in the TARDIS and got him away to safety.

After helping defeat a rogue Slitheen in Cardiff, Jack organised the army of volunteers that tried to stop the Daleks invading the Game Station. He was exterminated by the Daleks, but Rose brought him back to life. She used the power of the Time Vortex to make Jack live again — and now he is immortal! But to save her from that awful power, the Doctor had to take it into himself and regenerate into a new body. The TARDIS left the Game Station before Captain Jack could get back to it, but he was determined to meet up with the Doctor again.

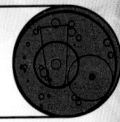

RELIVING THE PAST

Captain Jack used his Vortex manipulator to go back in time to look for the Doctor. He knew the Doctor would one day come to Cardiff to recharge the TARDIS using the time rift there, so that was where Jack planned to wait. He aimed for our time, but arrived in 1869. His Vortex Manipulator had burned out, so he had to wait over a hundred years for the Doctor.

In 1892, Captain Jack was on Ellis Island and got into a fight. He was shot through the heart — but he woke up again afterwards! Later he fell off a cliff, and one time he was trampled by horses. He died many times, during both world wars, and each time he came back from the dead. Having been saved by Rose, and given the power of the Time Vortex itself, Captain Jack was now indestructible.

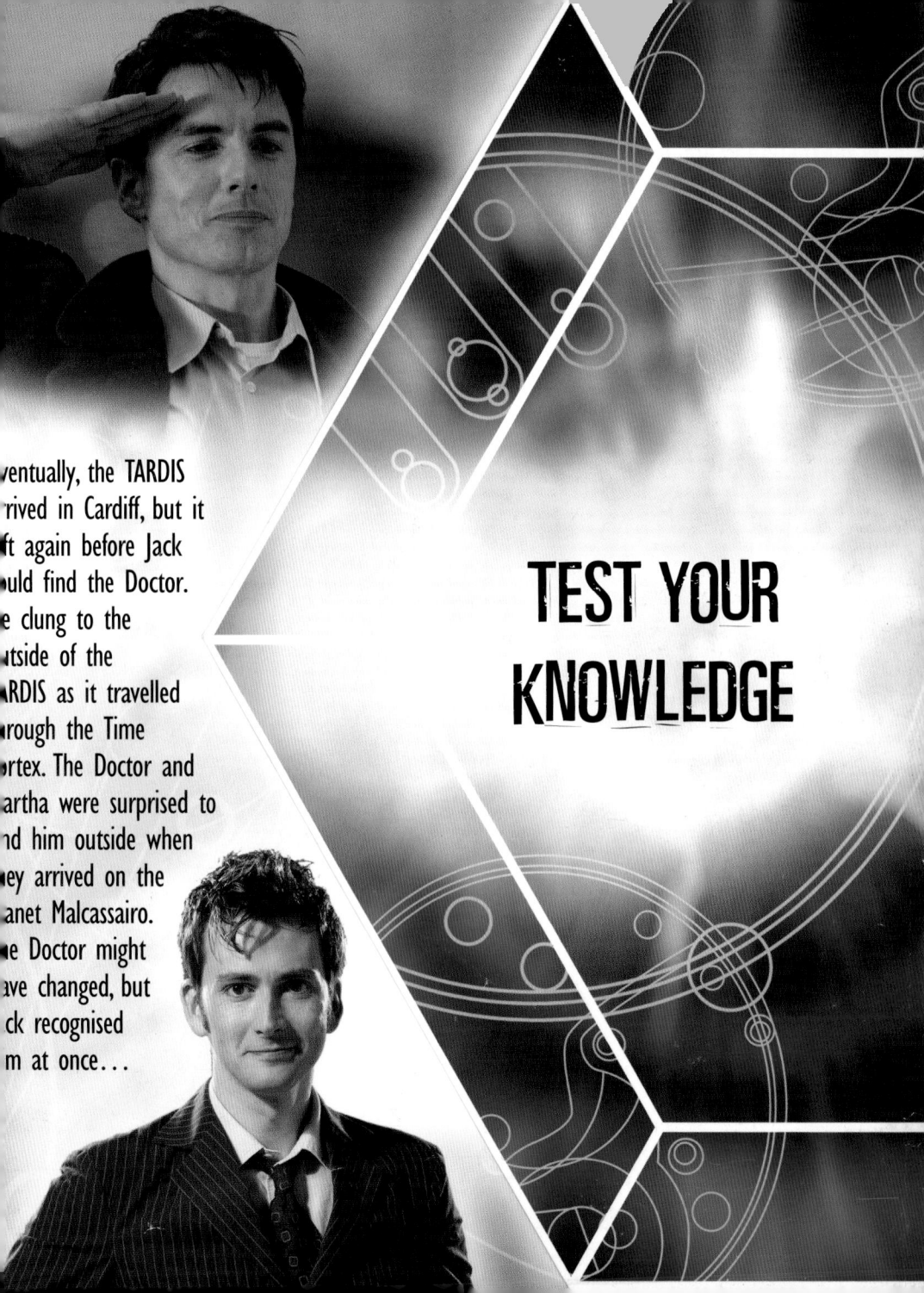

entually, the **TARDIS**
rived in Cardiff, but it
ft again before Jack
uld find the Doctor.
e clung to the
tside of the
RDIS as it travelled
rough the Time
rtex. The Doctor and
artha were surprised to
d him outside when
ey arrived on the
anet Malcassairo.
e Doctor might
ve changed, but
ck recognised
m at once...

TEST YOUR
KNOWLEDGE

JACK'S CAPABILITIES

INVISIBLE SPACESHIP

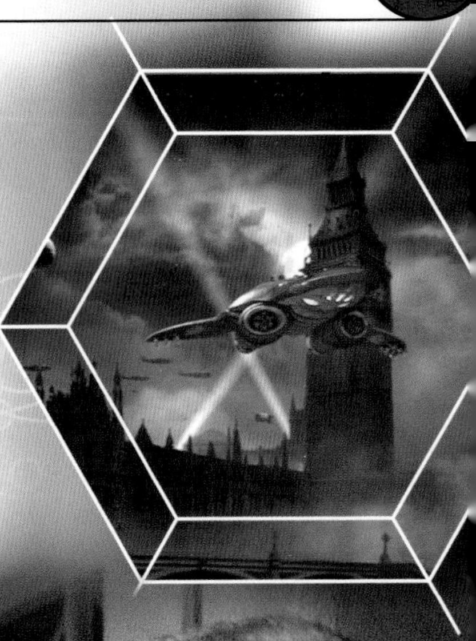

When Jack first met the Doctor and Rose he had a spaceship that had active camouflage so it could become invisible. He had it tethered to Big Ben, so he wouldn't lose it! The ship's computer could make Jack's favourite cocktail, and he had a teleport back to the ship which was security-keyed to his molecular structure. Using the ship's om-com system he could transmit his voice to anything with a speaker.

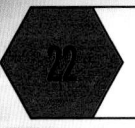

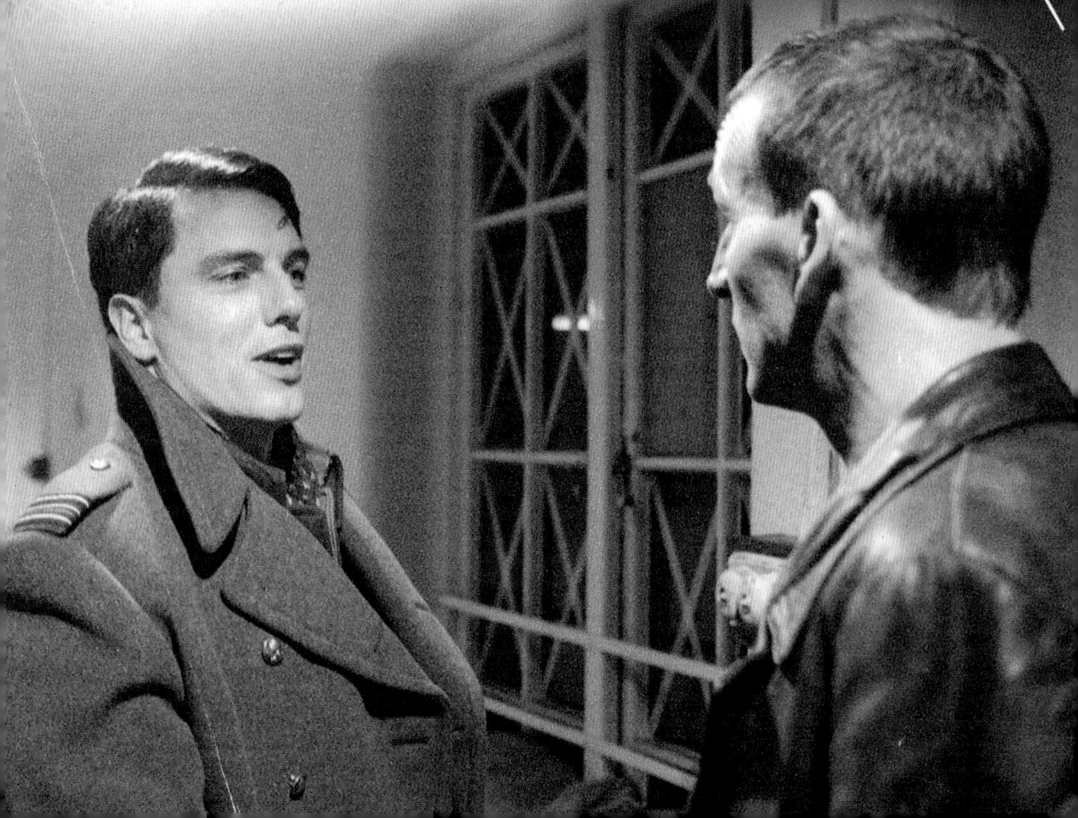

ORTEX MANIPULATOR

aptain Jack has a device on his wrist
lled a Vortex Manipulator. He's had it
nce he was a Time Agent, and it allows
m to travel in time. Or rather, it did
til it burned out. Its last working task
as to take Jack from the Game Station
the far future to Earth in the 21st
ntury. But he ended up stuck in
369 instead.

e Doctor is not impressed with
ck's Vortex Manipulator. He said that
mparing Jack's Manipulator to the
RDIS is like comparing a space
pper to a sports car!

HANDCUFFS

When the Doctor and his friends captured
Blon Fel Fotch Pasameer-Day Slitheen, Jack
lent the Doctor two rings that acted
like handcuffs. The Doctor wore one, the
Slitheen disguised as Margaret Blaine wore
the other one. Then, if she then moved
more than ten feet away from the Doctor
she would have been electrocuted.

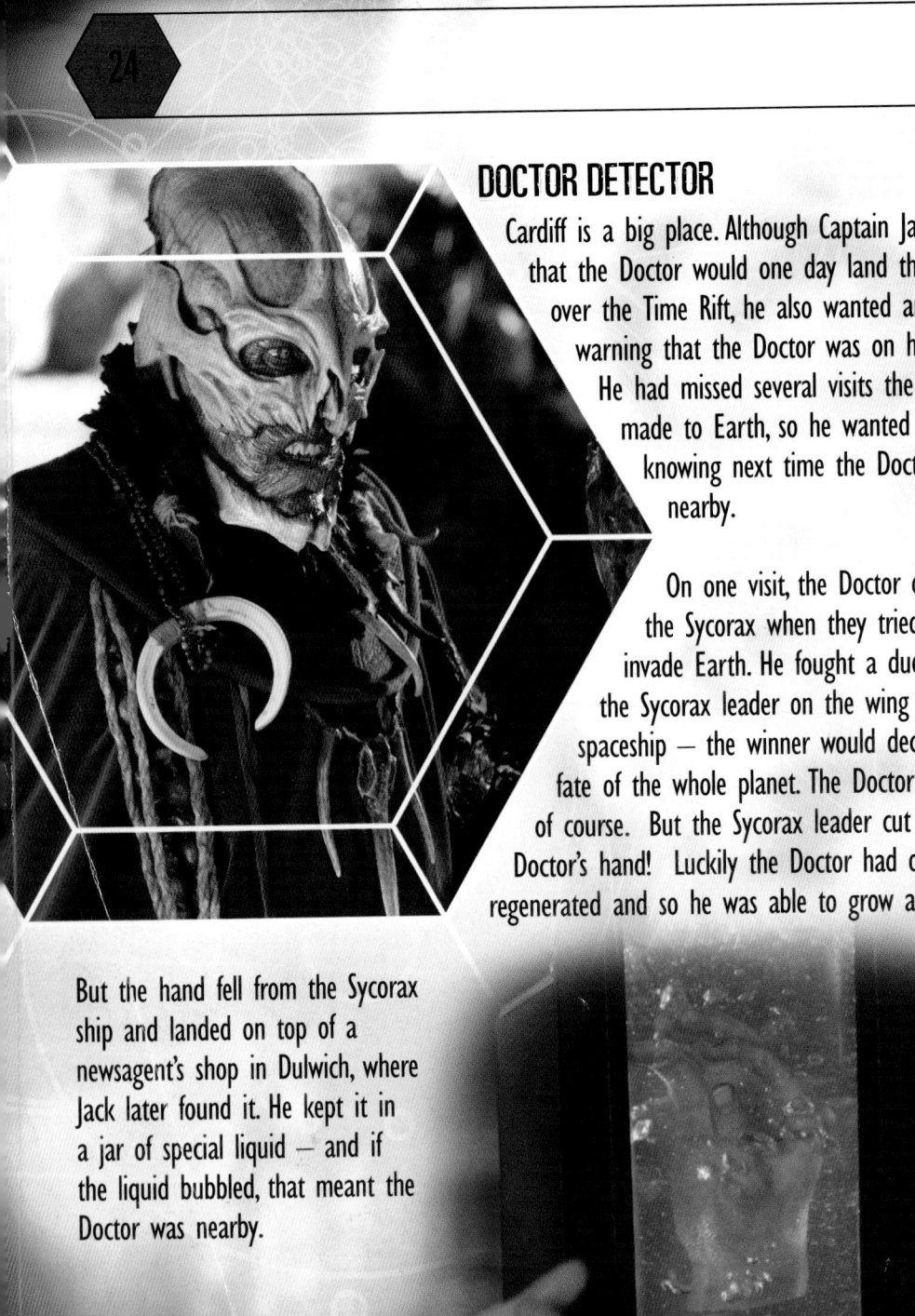

DOCTOR DETECTOR

Cardiff is a big place. Although Captain Jack knew that the Doctor would one day land the TARDIS over the Time Rift, he also wanted an early warning that the Doctor was on his way. He had missed several visits the Doctor made to Earth, so he wanted a way of knowing next time the Doctor was nearby.

On one visit, the Doctor defeated the Sycorax when they tried to invade Earth. He fought a duel against the Sycorax leader on the wing of their spaceship — the winner would decide the fate of the whole planet. The Doctor won, of course. But the Sycorax leader cut off the Doctor's hand! Luckily the Doctor had only just regenerated and so he was able to grow another on

But the hand fell from the Sycorax ship and landed on top of a newsagent's shop in Dulwich, where Jack later found it. He kept it in a jar of special liquid — and if the liquid bubbled, that meant the Doctor was nearby.

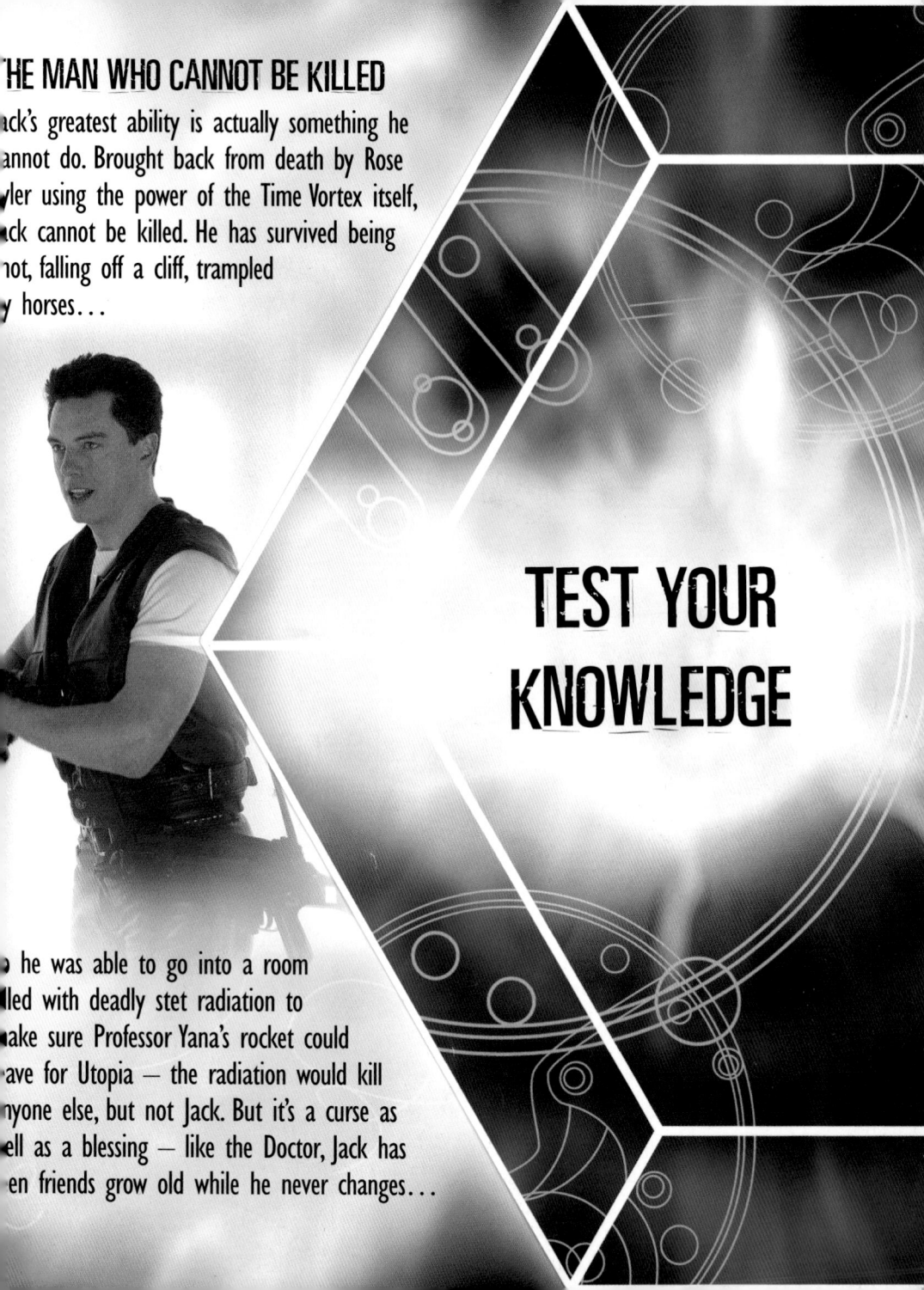

THE MAN WHO CANNOT BE KILLED

Jack's greatest ability is actually something he cannot do. Brought back from death by Rose Tyler using the power of the Time Vortex itself, Jack cannot be killed. He has survived being shot, falling off a cliff, trampled by horses...

So he was able to go into a room filled with deadly stet radiation to make sure Professor Yana's rocket could save for Utopia — the radiation would kill anyone else, but not Jack. But it's a curse as well as a blessing — like the Doctor, Jack has seen friends grow old while he never changes...

TEST YOUR KNOWLEDGE

MEETING THE DOCTOR AGAIN

Captain Jack waited for over a hundred years for the Doctor to come back and find him. Just as he might have expected, Jack's reunion with the Doctor was not quiet and safe. On the planet Malcassairo, Captain Jack, the Doctor and Martha Jones found the last survivors of humanity trying to get to a new home — Utopia.

But, even though he didn't know it, Professor Yana — the only man who could save humanity — was actually the Doctor's oldest enemy. He was another Time Lord called the Master. With his memory restored, and determined to cause trouble, the Master stole the TARDIS and left Jack and his friends stranded and under attack by savages...

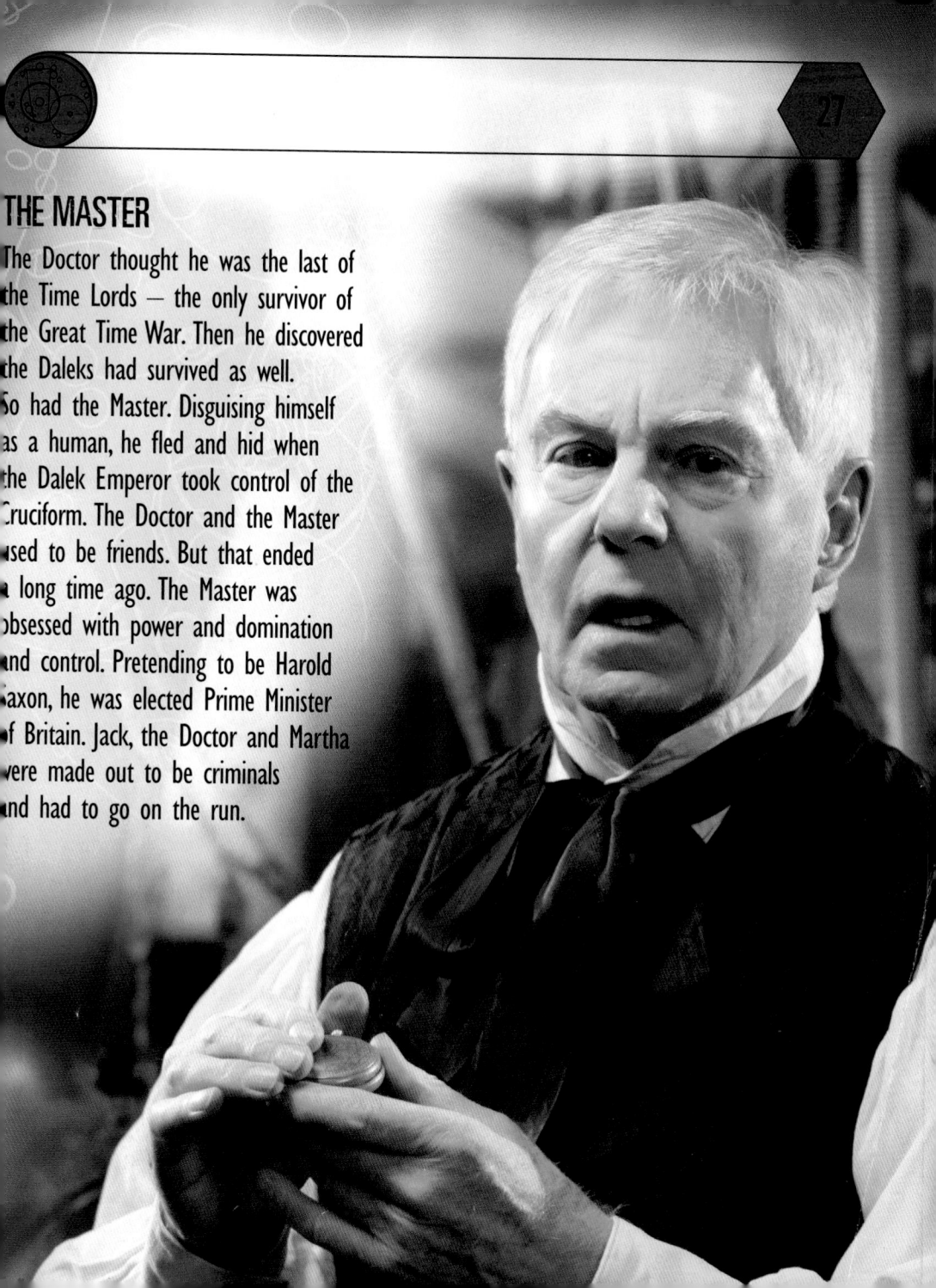

THE MASTER

The Doctor thought he was the last of the Time Lords — the only survivor of the Great Time War. Then he discovered the Daleks had survived as well. So had the Master. Disguising himself as a human, he fled and hid when the Dalek Emperor took control of the Cruciform. The Doctor and the Master used to be friends. But that ended a long time ago. The Master was obsessed with power and domination and control. Pretending to be Harold Saxon, he was elected Prime Minister of Britain. Jack, the Doctor and Martha were made out to be criminals and had to go on the run.

THE SPHERES

The Master claimed to have made contact with an alien race — metallic sphere creatures called the Toclafane. From the safety of the flying aircraft carrier Valiant, he brought six billion of the Spheres to invade Earth. Whole countries and continents of people were wiped out, and the survivors were enslaved. They were made to build great rocket ships that would wage war on the rest of the Universe. The Doctor and Jack were both held captive — only Martha could save the world.

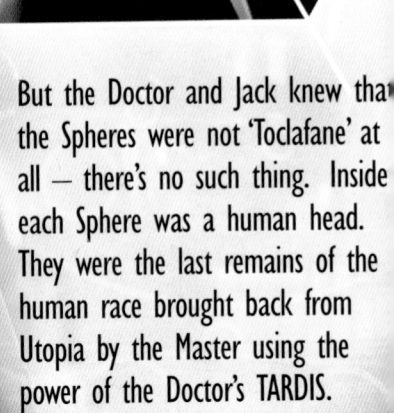

But the Doctor and Jack knew that the Spheres were not 'Toclafane' at all — there's no such thing. Inside each Sphere was a human head. They were the last remains of the human race brought back from Utopia by the Master using the power of the Doctor's TARDIS.

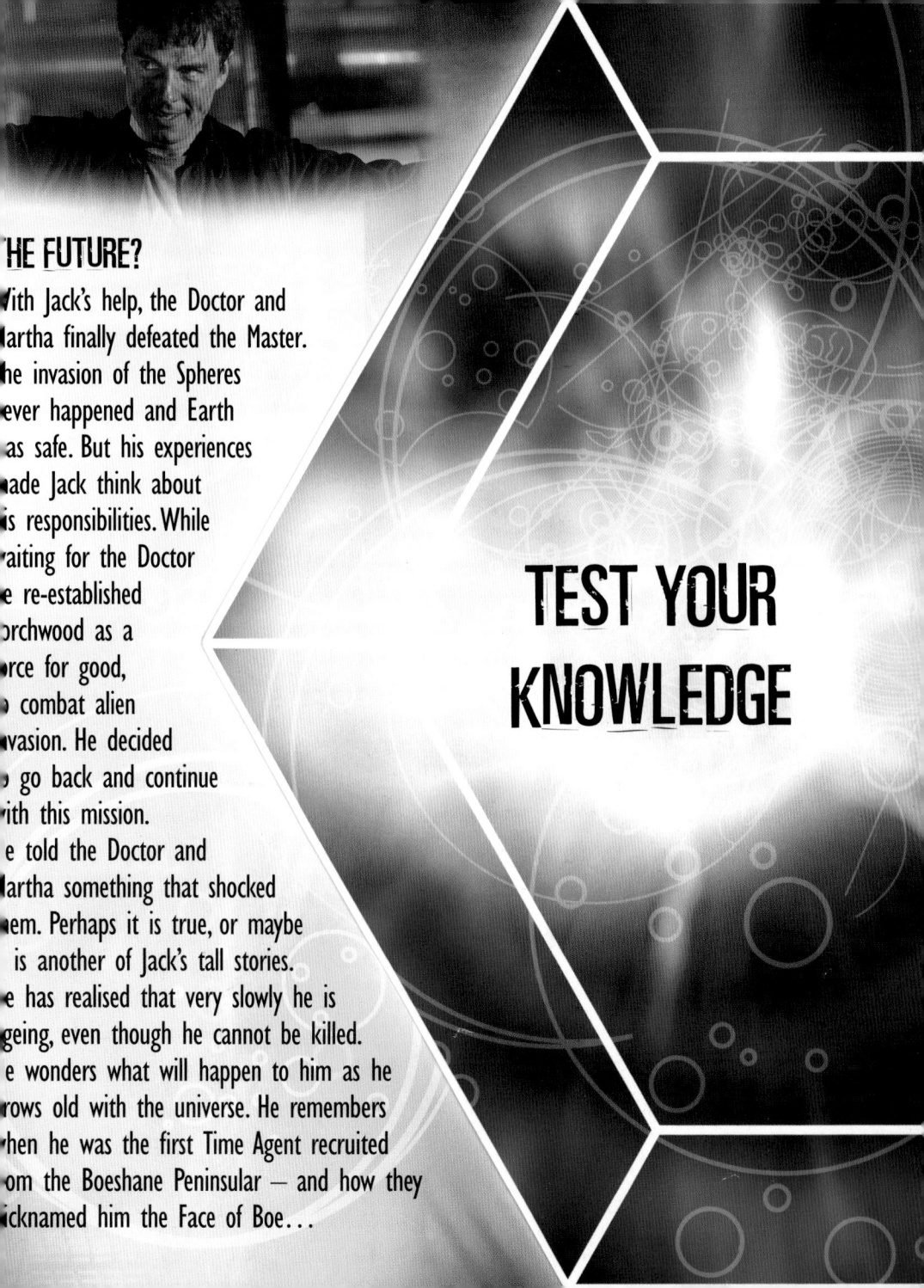

HE FUTURE?

With Jack's help, the Doctor and Martha finally defeated the Master. The invasion of the Spheres never happened and Earth was safe. But his experiences made Jack think about his responsibilities. While waiting for the Doctor he re-established Torchwood as a force for good, to combat alien invasion. He decided to go back and continue with this mission. He told the Doctor and Martha something that shocked them. Perhaps it is true, or maybe it is another of Jack's tall stories. He has realised that very slowly he is ageing, even though he cannot be killed. He wonders what will happen to him as he grows old with the universe. He remembers when he was the first Time Agent recruited from the Boeshane Peninsular — and how they nicknamed him the Face of Boe...

TEST YOUR KNOWLEDGE

ANSWERS

Meet Captain Jack Harkness
1 (b) 2 (a) 3 (b) 4 (c) 5 (c)

Captain Jack's Friends
1 (a) 2 (c) 3 (b) 4 (b) 5 (a)

Captain Jack's Enemies
1 (b) 2 (c) 3 (a) 4 (b) 5 (a)

The Lives and Times of Jack
1 (a) 2 (c) 3 (a) 4 (b) 5 (c)

Jack's Capabilities
1 (a) 2 (c) 3 (b) 4 (c) 5 (b)

Further Adventures of Jack
1 (c) 2 (b) 3 (b) 4 (a) 5 (b)